The Baseball-Bats

The Beginning

Written & Illustrated by
Philip Vaughn Murphy

AuthorHouse™
1663 Liberty Drive
Bloomington, IN 47403
www.authorhouse.com
Phone: 1-800-839-8640

Published by AuthorHouse 11/17/2014

ISBN: 978-1-4969-4750-5 (sc)
ISBN: 978-1-4969-5070-3 (hc)
ISBN: 978-1-4969-4751-2 (e)

Library of Congress Control Number: 2014919440

authorHOUSE®

This book is dedicated to my Mom and Dad, my wife Leah and daughters Rachel and Taylor for their support in all my artistic endeavors.

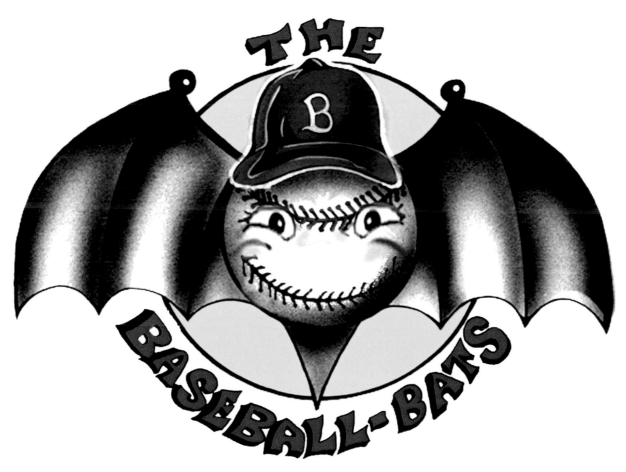

Another night descends on the city, and the bats that inhabit the upper beams of baseball stadiums around the country, awaken to the twinkle of stars and the sounds of pre-game warm-ups. Banners flutter in the evening breeze and the stands slowly fill with fans. Children's laughter can be heard over the hot-dog vendors, as they eagerly await the traditional, "Play ball!" from the home plate umpire.

These young bats enjoy and understood the game as well as their human counterparts. It's not . . . surprising . . . that this particular group of pups appreciates the game of baseball as they do . . . because . . . well . . . they resemble baseballs, and, I might add, play the game with great skill. The rafters of old ball parks are the only homes they know.

As the story goes, their mothers survived through the worst storm to pass through the area in years. However, something strange happened during that storm, something very strange indeed. Well let me tell you the story, as it was told to me . . .

The weatherman had called for thunderstorms, but not until later that night. It seemed the game would be finished before the bad weather arrived, even though threatening dark clouds were gathering over the stadium. Because of the forecast, the umpires decided to turn the lights on early, making the field brighter and safer for the players. Usually the lights came on automatically for night games.

As game time approached, the stadium gradually changed, from a semi-circle of gold, red, blue, and green sections, to a multicolored sea of fans. Some, who had probably heard the weather reports, wore hats and sweaters, in case of a sudden downpour. Others carried umbrellas, while many arrived in their usual summer attire scoffing at the weatherman and the unfriendly sky.

Forty bats had slept in the cavern for the winter, undisturbed by the everyday actions of the humans inhabiting the world above them. The warm quiet roost in which they spent the year, was a "nursery" full of expectant mothers huddled together awaiting the arrival of their young pups. It was nothing more than a long, narrow passage, ending in a hollow the size of a beach ball. The entrance was a hole on the rocky face of a cliff sloping to an oceans sandy shore.

Soon the new born would occupy the same small space, clinging to their mothers for the first few weeks of life. The cool, wet season was over and summer was about to arrive, welcoming the new brown bats. The males had migrated or found more suitable roosts for the winter, only to return in the spring when the pups were independent.

Jockeying for position along the ceiling, the mothers tried to avoid the strange unexpected bursts of light that disturbed their slumber.

Some days they awoke to sounds that vibrated through the rock, the footsteps and voices echoing from the world above them. They would stir sleepily, nuzzle a shoulder or wing, and then fall back into a deep sleep.

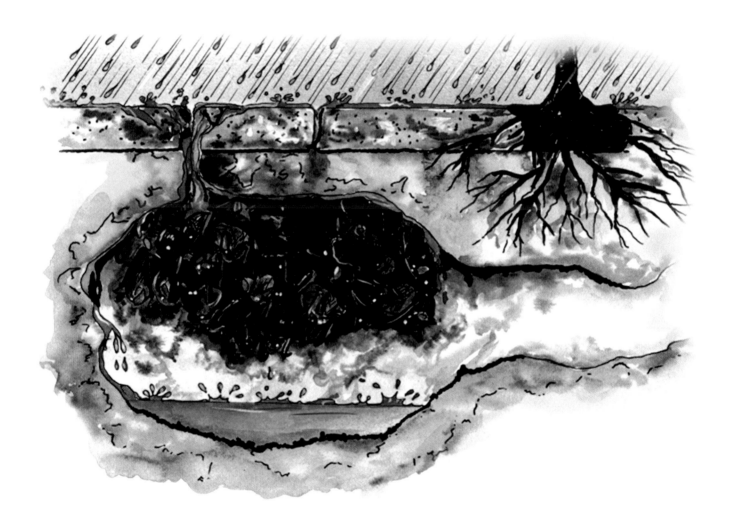

Today the roost felt damp and cold. An odd feeling filled the air. The offensive stream of bright flashing light, followed by a clap of thunder, vibrating through their tiny ears, was only the beginning of what was to be a very exciting night!

There was a buzz in the stands, as the fans rallied behind their home town heroes. The score in the second inning was 1—0, in favor of the home team. The chants of hot-dog, popcorn and soft drink vendors could be heard above the crowd, announcing the delights they offered. Boys and girls leaned on railings, waving team pennants while their parents sat, skillfully keeping one eye on the game and the other on their excited children.

As dusk slowly turned to night, the brilliance of the park lights washed a magical blue glow over whatever it touched. The only hints now, of unsettled weather, were the little dust devils still forming in the corners of the diamond. Paper cups and candy wrappers that had blown on to the field went spinning magically, up into the air.

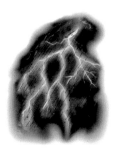

Dark clouds churned in the night sky above the stadium, invisible behind the lights glowing embrace.

Their three month hibernation passed quietly. One of the females, Scout, as she was known to the others, woke periodically and ventured outside to check the weather while the others slept. Upon returning she would wake the resting mothers or return to sleep herself, until her next weather check. She wasn't expecting a pup, but lived in the nursery, to help when the young were born.

That night, she awoke to cheeps, chirps and squeals of annoyance that filled the tiny roost. The cycle of hibernation had come to an abrupt end. Whatever had caused the commotion needed her immediate attention.

"Chuuurrr . . . Crrraaack!" flashed the light. Large amounts of water poured in, forming small rivulets along the upper surface of the nursery where the bats roosted.

Scout fluttered furiously, letting light taps of her wings and high pitch chirps, signal the danger they faced. They had no choice, but to flee the cavern to another roost for the mothers and their unborn pups.

The wind blew against the cliff face making the entrance unavailable for escape.

'Adult Brown Bats are only two to three inches long, too small to withstand the tempest that blew down that small tunnel.'

Scout found a different escape route. She would fly her brood through the small crack that had appeared above their roost. The same breach, the light and water used to rush into their home; they would use to rush out. They were hungry and weak after their long hibernation. Scout hoped their maternal instincts would be enough to carry them and their unborn pups to safety.

"Bats are hardy creatures, but were these bats brave enough to fly into the eye of a storm," she thought.

Sprinkles of rain started to fall. Fans donned their hats, and umbrellas blossomed like colored mushrooms throughout the stands. The miniature twisters continued to taunt the players, but the game rolled briskly along.

The fans were comfortably settled in their seats when,

"OH!" they gasped, surprised by a clap of thunder, drowning out all other sound.

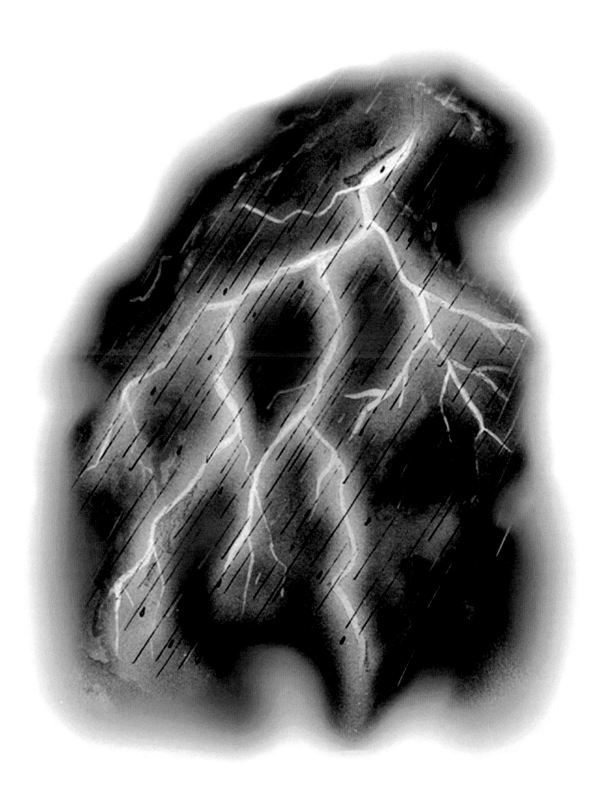

Players also jumped, then looked at one another wearing a broad smile that said,

"Hey, I saw you jump too!" happy in the fact, that he, wasn't the only one caught off-guard by the loud crack.

Then, as if the thunder had been warning, large drops of rain began to fall completely dousing fans and players alike. The only people spared from a soaking were the players sitting in the dugouts, protected from the wet weather. All they could do was sit and point, laughing at their teammates on the wet field, dripping from head to toe.

"Chuuurrr . . . Crrraaack!"

When the first brilliant bolt of lightning shattered the night sky, the umpires called a rain delay. Umbrellas closed as quickly as they had opened, allowing their owners to climb the stairs, and searching for the closest shelter from the sudden storm. Before long the stands returned to their original sections of color, as a sheet of water covered the diamond.

The wind and rain played supporting roles to the thunder and lightning that took center stage above the baseball diamond.

To hasten their escape the bats gathered in pairs, enabling one partner to help the other as they flew.

"Fly into the light!" Scout chirped to the mothers, now aware of their predicament. "It's our only way out!" she yelled, over the sound of the wind and rushing water.

The rivulets got bigger as the water splashed through the small hole that split the roof of their home.

"Chuuurrr . . . Crrraaack!"

"Bang . . . Crack-a-bang!" The lightning and thunder persisted with each blinding flash and deafening crack.

They spread their wings, and flapped them furiously to get the blood circulating after their long sleep. Shaking their tiny heads and blinking their eyes against the wind and rain, they each gave a thumbs up and burst through the tiny opening. With their chins buried into their chests, they flew aloft, pairs of tiny, flying mice, soaring into the unknown, driven by a strong desire to survive.

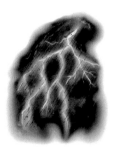

Meanwhile, fans ran, crouched under re-opened umbrellas as they ventured outside the ball park. The sidewalk shone like a mirror outside the stadium. The streetlights helped reflect all that occurred upon its surface.

"Chuuurrr . . . Crrraaack!" whipped a jagged fork of lightning, briefly erasing any reflections that formed between the large drops, dancing like shards of glass, and the sidewalks' crystal gleam.

"Bang . . . Crack-a-bang!" clapped the thunder.

People used whatever they could to cover their heads as they ran to cars, buses and street cars, eager to start their journey home. Some used game programs, while others pulled their soggy sweaters or jackets high over their heads. Other brave souls decided to run from one available shelter to the next, like mice, zigzagging their way to a chosen destination, stopping in safe nooks to check for potential dangers along the way.

Slow moving beams of light appeared around the stadium. They too moved in pairs, illuminating the blanket of rain that blocked their progress. As more beams came to life, a woven web of light was born. The number of pedestrians that dashed from the stadium diminished, while the web of light, that now covered the parking lot, grew larger and larger.

In all the commotion, the fluttering wave of black that shot up through the crack in the sidewalk went unnoticed. Up along the wall of the stadium they flew, Scout leading, eagerly beckoning them onward and upward, to whatever lay on the other side of the cold wet wall.

Up, up, they flew, as large drops of water pelted against their bodies. They flapped their wet leather-like wings vigorously to gain more altitude.

"Bang . . . Crack-a-bang!" roared the thunder.

Scout could barely see the top of the wall as she led her band up along its face.

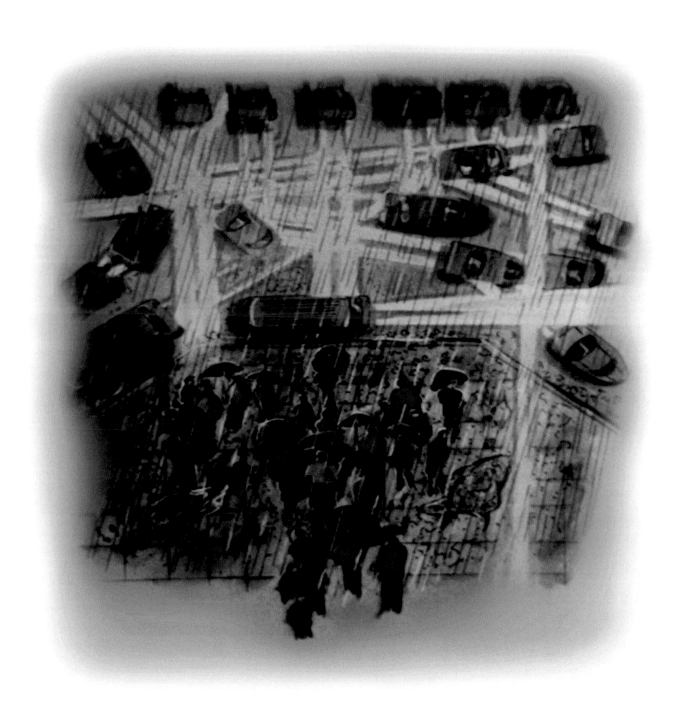

Inside, between the bursts of lightning, the stadium lights illuminated the rain. Six men in blue rain coats, hurriedly unrolled a large black tarp over the diamond, protecting it from the storm. Two others, carried containers, and collected whatever lay on the field.

"This structure resembled the rock face that held the entrance to the nursery," she thought, desperately trying to find an opening in the rock, while squinting tightly to avoid the rain. A bolt of lightning danced wildly across the black sky.

"Chuuurrr . . . Crrraaack!" it snapped as it lit up the night.

"Look!" one of the younger mothers yelled flapping her wings faster to take the lead. "There . . . just up ahead!" she shouted.

"Bang . . . crack-a-bang!" rolled the thunder.

"A few more feet, we're almost there!" the mother shouted, spurring her friends on over the loud thunderclap.

The rain showed no mercy as it splattered their small faces. The higher they flew, the heavier their little bodies became. As the last glow of lightning surrendered to the night, a definite line formed, separating the sky from the top of the smooth rock face.

"I can't! . . . I can't make it!" yelled an exhausted voice from the rear of the flying convoy.

"No!" yelled Scout, who had heard the weary plea and flown back to help. "You'll make it with the rest of us!" she said, determination in her face as she spoke to the faltering mother.

"It's no use, my wings are too heavy!" she cried.

Scout positioned herself above the bat, and in a scissors-like fashion wrapped her legs around the mother's waist.

Straining to look upward, she witnessed the rest of her tiny friends fly over the top of the concrete wall, to what she hoped was safety. The weight of the mother drained her strength. Silently she apologized for the weakness in her weather beaten wings. She took comfort in the fact that she had given the others a fighting chance at surviving. She fell limp, and gave in to the forces of nature. Gravity and the torrential rain forced them both toward the ground. The thunder roared and lightning filled the sky once more, as they plummeted together, to the mirror like sidewalk below.

Inside the stadium, just under the lip of the of the wall, the tired group hung, grasping tightly to whatever foot hold they could find, gathering strength for the next step in their journey. The heavy rain fell away from where they rested.

The mother, who had been the first over the top, realized that Scout was missing. She chirped to her closest companion and without considering the danger, both bats spread their wings and catapulted, back over the wall. Turning their tiny heads from side to side, both bats sent out beams of ultrasonic sound, to locate their friends. The force of the rain increased their decent. They used their wings and tail membranes like parachutes to break the currents of air that streamed passed them on their downward search.

Suddenly, they received a weak echo and bravely swooped in the direction of the returning sounds.

One by one the remaining bats slowly made their way to the upper surface of the ledge. Using their wings as protection against the wind and rain, they peered down, in hope of their friends return.

All they saw was rain, rain and more rain.

Lightning, "Chuuurrr . . . Crrraaack!" lit up the sky, followed by a thunderclap. "Bang . . . crack-a-bang!"

Then, a strange shape began to take form. Two bats flapping their wings wildly, their feet holding firm to Scout's thumbs burst up from the abyss. An excited cheer rose up from the group as the two heroes gently laid Scout on the wet bluff, her legs, still held valiantly around the waist of the young mother she had saved.

Tired but unhurt, after their heroic escapade, they again took refuge under the rim of the wall. They took comfort once more in the warmth of the whole group.

The rain continued to fall. The wind changed direction. The cold rain drops soon targeted the ledge where they hung.

"Chuuurrr . . . Crrraaack!" blazed a fork of lightning.

The thunder rumbled "Boom . . . crack-a-bang!"

"Was there no end to this storm?" Scout wondered. No matter how fast or how far they fled, the wind and rain always found them, relentless in their pursuit.

"**D**own there!" she chirped to the other bats. "We'll have to look for refuge down there!" she said, gesturing with a wing toward the large black diamond shape that lay on the ground below them. The other wing she kept folded around her body, a shield from the rain. The others squinted in the direction she had pointed, their eyes straining over the wings protecting their tiny bodies.

"It seems worse down there," answered one.

"And we're not sure what we'll find," added another, her voice filled with concern.

To save our strength, we can glide down." said Scout encouragingly "but, we'll have to find shelter quickly." she chirped, wondering if it was possible without drowning or being beaten into the ground by the rain.

Another bat, the mother whom Scout had rescued, interrupted. "It seems to me that if we hang around here discussing all the reasons why we shouldn't move on, we won't have a bat's chance in hades of surviving the night." She paused, turning her head from side to side, avoiding the rain and noting the reactions to her scolding tone. They all looked stunned at her take charge attitude.

She continued, "I'm with Scout. We've come this far, I'm not giving up now! We have more than just ourselves to think about here. I'm going to give my child every chance to survive," she paused and took a breath, "or die trying."

Well, she had challenged their motherhood and drawn a line in the sand. All they had to do now was cross it.

Suddenly, a voice rose above the storm, like a bugle blast on a battle field.

"WELL . . . ARE WE MICE OR BATS?" it trumpeted.

With that, they leapt down from under their perch, out into the unknown, like a squadron of jet planes, setting their sights on victory.

"Chuuurrr . . . Crrraaack!" The playing field came into full focus as they flew closer to the ground.

"Try to stay together . . . and in . . . tight formation." shouted Scout, hoping to be heard over the storm. By this time, they had to depend on their keen eyesight; their echolocation was a confused mass of signals, due to exhaustion.

"Good luck." she added, knowing they'd need it.

The lightning flashed on cue freezing the ground crew in mid-stride, like statues as if a huge camera had taken their picture.

"Boom . . . crack-a-boom!"

It seemed as though the stadium itself cringed with every roll of thunder.

"That's it!" the foreman shouted. "Everyone inside, NOW!"

Eight blue figures ran for cover, instantly abandoning whatever they were doing at the time. They didn't need to be told, twice.

The storm had succeeded in chasing anything that moved from the stadium.

"Chuuurrr . . . Crrraaack!" flashed the lightning. It was too busy above the ball park, beating its chest in triumph, to notice the small band of determined little bats swooping down in defiance.

"Bang . . . crack-a-boom!" it blasted.

Wrinkled in several areas, the black tarp completely covered the diamond. The ground's staff had made certain, anything with a lock or latch had been secured against the weather.

The bats descended in a low arc, soaring in toward the black diamond that lay before them. The wind whipped around the high walls of the stadium in all directions, a tempest in a teapot. It tugged at the corners of the tarp, blowing under it. To the bats flying just above, it resembled waves on water. Their instincts told them to avoid the black mass, and search on.

"Something . . . dead . . . ahead . . ." Scout struggled to speak, "a large . . . c . . . cavern, I can't quite . . . make out . . . f . . . fly for that opening!" It was difficult; her words were smothered by the force of the wind and rain. Fortunately, the others had understood her garbled instructions and flew for the large oblong recess.

It was as if they had flown into another dimension. They hung together along the ceiling, their backs against the rear wall. The rain spread like a sheet before them. Behind it, the thunder and lightning danced on.

"Chuuurrr . . . Crrraaack!"

"Bang . . . Crack-a-boom!"

A brown canvas bag hung on the side wall of the long recess. Scout went to investigate. Circling, she patted it with her wings. It was quite dry, and fastened in the front. A small wrinkle in the flap gave access to the inside. Letting the others rest, she took a thumb hold below the opening and with her strong shoulders pulled herself up, over and into the bag.

The bag made of thick rough material, held several harmless, white objects. They were round with lines of fiber on them. Her wish had been answered. The inside was dark warm and dry.

Upon her return, Scout excitedly informed the others of her discovery. Before long they were clumsily climbing, one after the other, into the canvas cavern, taking refuge in the warm little nooks the white spheres naturally formed between each other. Their quest had finally come to a successful end, or so it seemed. Content in their new home, they closed their eyes and took a hard earned . . . . bat nap. There they waited out the storm, forty bats, catching forty winks.

The bag looked no different. It still hung securely on the wall. Outsiders would never have guessed that after acquiring its new tenants, it now stowed balls . . . . and bats!

It seemed the storm's attention, now centered solely on the baseball diamond. The bacon frying sound the rain made as it beat down upon the black tarp could be heard from the bats dry shelter.

In the excitement of her discovery, Scout had not noticed the long rake and shovel, leaning against the wall, next to the bag of balls. The ground crew had left them in their hasty retreat.

41

"Chuuurrr . . . Crrraaack!" Lightning jumped along the rake's metal prongs, which shone like jagged teeth, searching for prey. With each gust of wind, both shovel and rake inched along the wall, eventually toppling to the ground.

The shovel landed on the cement floor with a "KLANK!" The rake fell with a muffled, "THUMPH" its teeth clawing the outside of the canvas bag.

"Chuuurrr . . . Crrraaack!"

"Bang . . . Crack-a-boom!"

The lightning and thunder appeared together as the storm approached. The jagged forks of light felt the ground, like searching hands.

"Snnaapp . . . Chuuurrr . . . Crrraaack!" a wisp of bright light took hold, weaving between the prongs of the rake and dancing wildly around the canvas bag. Without warning, the sleeping bats felt a surge of energy raise the hair on their backs, curl their lips and tickle their toes. A wave of electricity ran over their bodies, from the tips of their tiny noses to the ends of their pointed little tails. It seemed to last forever. They held desperately to the leather spheres, digging their feet and thumbs into the red stitching that surrounded them, their eyes closed tight.

"Bang . . . Crack-a-boom!" Suddenly the light released its grip on their bodies, as if obeying the thunderous command. The bats slumped over, completely stunned.

The storm had taken its toll. They had out run the wind and the rain, but the searching fingers of light had not given up so easily. Too afraid to return to sleep, they cowered in their little nooks, unable to move, their security gone with the last flash of light.

Many sounds broke the silence of the roost the following afternoon. Scout, listened, but the sounds she searched for had gone. No rain. No wind. No thunder. When her eyes adjusted to the small rays of light that perforated the canvas, she realized the light that had held them in its grasp was also gone. The others stirred, turning their heads carefully from side to side, not knowing what to expect. About the experience of the night before, not a word was spoken.

"They had all been so tired. Was it just a bad dream they'd shared?" Scout thought, unwilling to face the truth herself. "Well, they had survived the ordeal and that's what mattered."

Voices grew louder as footsteps moved closer to their roost. The bats remained as quiet as church mice, inside their canvas cave.

"These should do." a voice said. "Take third and I'll hit you some grounders."

The bag shifted with a jolt as it was lifted from its hook. The unseen figure jogged onto the damp, sunlit field unaware of the cheeps and chirps of annoyance that came from inside it.

Bats rolled over balls and balls over bats, until the player dropped the bag unceremoniously to the ground. Light immediately flooded in, as the canvas cover flipped open.

"**F**ly!" Scout yelled. "Fly!"

To the players' surprise, a swarm of tiny brown bats fluttered wildly from inside the ball bag. Some bounced off his chest; others glanced off his arm, in a desperate attempt to flee. Both surprised players stood in shock, scratching their heads as they witnessed the little stowaways, flying into the afternoon sun, toward the darkest spot they could find, the stadium rafters.

Weeks later, after that eventful night, the males returned to an abandoned nursery. To their surprise, they found the females in a comfortable roost among the rafters of the old baseball stadium, thirty-nine pups clutching tightly to their mothers, all looking strong and healthy, with one notable exception. Their bodies resembled tiny white baseballs.

With their mouths open wide, the bewildered fathers hung from the opposite rafter.

"I . . . I don't know what to say." one stammered, his eyes as big as saucers.

"I'm completely SHOCKED!" said another.

A secretive smile slowly formed on the face of each mother. Scout, who rocked as she hung, stopped her knitting, lowered her head and removed her spectacles. Holding her glasses in one wing, she pointed toward the astonished father, who had unwittingly chosen the right word.

"**S**HOCKED! Yep. That's about how we figured it too," she chuckled.

. . . And that, my young friends, is the story as I know it. The males from that first nursery migrated the following winter, roosting in baseball stadiums all across the country. "The Baseball Bats," as they are known today, sleep by day, but at night, long after the lights have gone out and the stadiums are quiet, they play the great game of baseball.

So, the next time you go to a baseball game, take a good look up into the rafters of the stadium. If you notice something round and white high in the beams, look a little harder to see if it has wings.

Printed in the United States
By Bookmasters